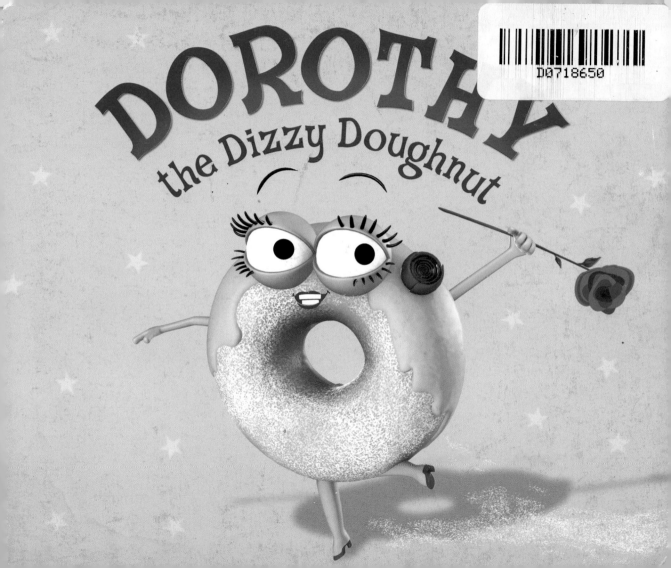

# DOROTHY
## the Dizzy Doughnut

**I**f there was one thing **Dorothy the Doughnut LOVED**, it was dancing.

She knew all the names...

The **waltz**...

the **tango**...

the **foxtrot**...

Even the **monster mash** and **jive**.

But Dorothy was a **TERRIBLE** dancer.

She had no rhythm.

She had two left feet.

And she wasn't really
the right **shape** for dancing.

You see, Dorothy was a doughnut, so everything about her was round.

**VERY** round, with a great big hole in the **middle**!

And when she danced, Dorothy dusted everyone with sugar.

But not only that...
Being the shape she was, she was clumsy.

**REALLY CLUMSY** would be the best way to put it.

**S**he sang as she bumped her way around the kitchen. And this made Brian the Bread Bin quite cross.

"Do stop it, Dorothy!" he boomed. **"CAN'T YOU SEE YOU'RE A TERRIBLE DANCER?"**

Everyone gasped. They knew Dorothy was an awful dancer, but it wasn't right to hurt her feelings like that.

Tina the Teapot said quickly, "I think what Brian means...
is... is that you might like some dancing **lessons**."

"Practice makes perfect!" added Josie the Jam Jar.

"Oh, that would be wonderful!" cried Dorothy.
And she did a little pirouette on the spot.

The next morning, a notice appeared on the sitting-room door.

"Come on in, Dorothy!" said Molly the Milk Jug, steering Dorothy to the front of the class.

The dancing teacher was Tina the Teapot.
Dorothy smiled a big, sugary smile.
She looked at her classmates.

Everyone in the class was identical... and tiny... in their tutus and dancing shoes.

Free
dancing
lessons!
Step
inside!

Dorothy counted.
"One... two... ten... twenty.
**SO MANY** tiny Housemites, and
with eight legs each," she giggled.
"That's **HUNDREDS** of feet to
compete with!"

"It's lucky I'm such a good dancer!" Dorothy decided.

And, to prove it, she launched into her favourite bit from *Swan Lake*.

She **jumped** and **rolled**...

and rolled again.

Then **flounced** and **kicked** and **jived**...

She **swerved** and **tripped**...

and **sprang** and **skipped**...

until she was
completely **exhausted**.

Dorothy finished with a flourish,
flushed with delight and excitement.

But everyone else was **squashed**...

or **bashed**...

or **bruised**...

or **cracked**...

or **chipped**.

Dorothy didn't notice.
She was waiting for the applause.

But there **was** no applause.

Just a terrible silence.

Then a great tearful wail went up.
It wasn't applause – it was crying!

# "WAAAAH!"

"We came here to learn how to dance!" they squeaked.
"Not to be flattened by an... an elephant!"

"I am **NOT** an elephant!" snapped Dorothy.
"I'm a doughnut. A very **SWEET** little doughnut, in fact."

"A very big, **CLUMSY** doughnut!"
replied a Housemite.

**N**ow, that was a **horrible** thing to say. Poor Dorothy was **SO** upset.

She turned and looked at her reflection in Tina's shiny side. It didn't help that it made her look even wider than she was...

About six times wider and shorter!

"You're right," sighed Dorothy, in a tiny voice.

"I'm just a big, clumsy doughnut. And I'll **never** be able to dance!"

All the tiny Housemites felt sorry for Dorothy.
Even the horrible one. But, rather than say anything,
they all tiptoed out of the room.

Molly the Milk Jug put her arm round Dorothy
(well, as far round as she could reach!).

"Never mind," she said. "How about a nice cup of tea?"

Dorothy brightened immediately.
"I just want to dance," she cried.

Then Molly had an idea.

"What you need," Molly said brightly,
"is a partner. A dancing partner! Someone to
point you in the right direction."

*But who would want to dance with a doughnut?*

"How about me?" added a deep, silky voice.

It was Roger the Rolling Pin, all dressed up
and ready to party.

Dorothy didn't need asking twice.
"Count me in!" she smiled.

So Roger did.

"One, two, three... one, two, three... waltz!"

From somewhere the music started,
or was it just in their heads?
They whirled and swirled and glided...

Soft, **round Dorothy**

and tall, **thin Roger.**

and the foxtrot...

They danced the waltz...                    and the tango...

and finally the moonwalk...

just as the moon came up.

Then into the timewarp...

No one got squashed...
or bashed...
or bruised...

No one got showered...
or powdered... with sugar!

"Crumbs!" said Brian the Bread Bin.
"With Roger, Dorothy is a **WONDERFUL** dancer!"

Dorothy was enjoying herself **SO** much!

Faster and faster she twirled:

# Wheeeeeeeeeeee!

And each time she twirled,
Roger caught her.

Except once...

"Is that what they call hula dancing?" wondered Tina.

"I suppose it might be," replied Molly.

"But in a very roundabout way!"

Come and play hide and seek with us at...

www.hoohahouse.com